Disney

MEET THE
ROBINSONS

The Chapter Book

Meet the Robinsons: The Chapter Book

Copyright © 2007 Disney Enterprises, Inc.

RADIO FLYER is a registered trademark of Radio Flyer, Inc. and is used with permission.

Printed in the United States of America.

www.harpercollinschildrens.com

ISBN-10: 0-06-112474-5 — ISBN-13: 978-0-06-112474-7

❖

First Edition

"This area's not secure! Get in!" Wilbur Robinson, a slick kid with a lightning bolt on his T-shirt, grabbed Lewis and pulled him under the blanket. *This is strange*, thought Lewis, as he huddled next to his Memory Scanner with some kid he had never seen before in his life.

"Have you been approached by a tall man in a bowler hat?" Wilbur asked sharply. He had traveled back in time to this science fair to find the genius invention-making kid named Lewis and a tall man in a bowler hat (aka Bowler Hat Guy).

"What?" asked a bewildered Lewis.

"Hey, I'll ask the questions around here!"

Wilbur was getting annoyed. The situation was urgent.

"Okay. Good-bye." Lewis began to back away. He thought Wilbur was crazy.

"All right. Didn't want to pull rank on you, but you forced my hand. Special Agent Wilbur Robinson of the TCTF." There wasn't really a TCTF, but desperate times called for desperate measures. Wilbur had to lie. A little. But it was for Lewis's own good (and Wilbur's, too).

"What?" asked a bewildered Lewis again.

"Time Continuum Task Force," Wilbur Robinson explained. "I'm here to protect you. Now. Tall man. Bowler hat. Approached you?"

"No," Lewis replied. "Why?"

Wilbur sighed. "I could lose my badge for this. He's a suspect in a robbery."

"What did he steal?" asked Lewis, his eyes widening.

"A Time Machine." Aha! That got Lewis's attention, all right.

"A *what*?"

"I've traced him back to this time, and my

informants say he's after you," Wilbur replied.

"Me?!" Wilbur could tell that Lewis was shocked. "Why me?"

There wasn't time for Wilbur to explain everything to Lewis. It had all begun in the future, when Wilbur had left his family's garage door open after taking out the trash. Unfortunately for Wilbur, this allowed Bowler Hat Guy to enter the garage, steal one of the Robinsons' two Time Machines, and travel back in time to Lewis's science fair.

This created a big problem for Wilbur. He knew that the stolen Time Machine meant being grounded for the rest of his life. And Wilbur's only way to avoid that was to *never*, *ever* let his parents find out that a) the Time Machine had been stolen and b) it was his fault.

So Wilbur had devised a clever plan. He had followed Bowler Hat Guy in the other Time Machine and would return both machines to the future before his parents found out.

But for now, Wilbur had to deal with Lewis. The kid had invented a Memory Scanner. This made Wilbur nervous. He recognized that Memory

Scanner—from the future. He had to make sure nothing happened to it, or the future could be in jeopardy!

Meanwhile, Lewis was really confused by Wilbur and the whole idea of a creepy Bowler Hat Guy.

"Just worry about your little science gizmo and leave the 'perp' to me," Wilbur told Lewis. Then Wilbur ducked back out into the room and went looking for Bowler Hat Guy. Now there were two big things at stake: the Time Machine . . . and Lewis's Memory Scanner.

Chapter 2

Wilbur scanned the gymnasium for Bowler Hat Guy. He thought he spotted him and accidentally tackled some kid with a solar system model. Oops.

"All right, Lewis," said Mr. Willerstein, the science teacher. He turned to the crowd and introduced Lewis.

Lewis uncovered his Memory Scanner. Dr. Krunklehorn, the wacky judge from Inventco Labs, gasped.

"Oh!" she cried. "It's shiny!"

Lewis smiled as he put on the headset, typed in a date that he wanted to remember (the day his mother had left him on the orphanage steps), and started the machine. "It'll just take a second to get the turbines going," he said as a fan started to whirl.

Wilbur looked across the gym hopefully. It looked as if Lewis was off to a good start, and Bowler Hat Guy was nowhere in sight. It seemed that all was going well.

Then Wilbur spotted Bowler Hat Guy. He really was there, and he and his nasty robotic bowler hat, Doris, had done something to ruin Lewis's Memory Scanner.

"Lewis!" Wilbur shouted. "Wait!"

It was too late. Lewis had already started up the machine. Wilbur cringed as he watched the fan fly off the Memory Scanner and hit the lights on the ceiling. Sparks flew from the lights, setting off the fire sprinklers. Soon one boy's volcano experiment erupted, spewing orange goo all over. A little girl's fire ants escaped and started biting the school's coach. Another girl's frogs escaped and hopped all over the room. Soon the gym was in complete chaos.

"Let's calm down!" Mr. Willerstein shouted.

Lewis was horrified. "I'm sorry, I'm so sorry . . . !" He ripped off his headset and ran out the door.

"Wait! Lewis!" Wilbur called as he raced after him.

A few minutes later, after everyone else had evacuated the gymnasium, Bowler Hat Guy crept out of hiding with Doris on his head.

"Come, my dear," said the tall, mustached villain. "Our future awaits. *Mwa-hahaha-haha!*" Then he grabbed Lewis's Memory Scanner and dashed away.

So far, their evil plan was working perfectly. Unfortunately for Wilbur, things kept getting worse.

Chapter 3

This is not good, Wilbur thought as he watched Lewis from behind a wall on the roof of the orphanage.

Lewis was ripping out page after page of invention plans from his notebook. He wadded up the page with the Memory Scanner diagram into a ball and threw it across the roof.

Wilbur had to do something. He knew that Lewis had to keep those plans and fix the Memory Scanner so that the future wouldn't be altered.

He tossed the paper back at Lewis.

"Coo! Coo!" he said.

"Would you quit that, please?" Lewis shouted, throwing the paper back. "I know you're not a pigeon!"

Wilbur ran over to Lewis with the page. "Take this back to the science fair and fix that Memory Scanner."

"Stop!" Lewis cried. "Get away from me."

"Maybe you've forgotten," Wilbur said. "I'm a time cop from the future." But as Wilbur flashed his "badge," Lewis grabbed it.

"This is a coupon for a tanning salon. You're a fake!" Lewis said.

Wilbur gulped. Busted. "Okay, you got me. I'm not a cop," he said. "But I really am from the future, and there really is this Bowler Hat Guy." Wilbur continued, "He stole a Time Machine, came to the science fair, and ruined your project."

"My project didn't work because I'm no good," Lewis shot back. "You're not from the future.

You're crazy!"

"I am not crazy!" said Wilbur. This was not going according to his plan—not at all.

"Oh, yeah?" snapped Lewis. "Prove it!"

Prove it, huh? Wilbur knew what he had to do. He reached out and grabbed Lewis.

"Hey! Let go of me!" Lewis shouted.

"Okay," said Wilbur. *You ask for it; you get it.* Wilbur launched a shrieking Lewis over the edge of the orphanage roof and watched until he stopped falling—*Kathunk!*—in midair. Then Wilbur hopped off the roof after him.

Wilbur pressed an invisible button, and a Time

Machine appeared around them. He yanked a lever, and the vehicle blasted toward the sky.

"What is this?" Lewis shouted. "Where are we going?"

"To the future!" Wilbur shouted back. Wilbur expertly piloted the amazing vehicle, and suddenly the Time Machine emerged in the future. Wilbur enjoyed watching Lewis's face as the boy scientist got his first glimpse of the incredible city beneath them. It was unlike anything Lewis had ever seen. A woman shot past in a flying car, and below, people traveled in giant floating bubbles.

A grin spread across Wilbur's face. "Is this proof enough for ya?" he asked.

"Is it ever!" was all Lewis could say.

"Next stop: science fair," Wilbur announced, "to fix your Memory Scanner."

But Lewis saw other possibilities.

"I'm not gonna fix that stupid Memory Scanner," he said flatly. Why should he? This Time Machine could take him back to meet his mother.

"The answer is not a Time Machine," argued Wilbur. "It's this." He handed the crumpled Memory

Scanner plans to Lewis.

Both boys were determined to get their way. They struggled for control of the Time Machine, each trying to take command. Wilbur thought he had the upper hand.

"You're twelve, and I'm thirteen," said Wilbur. "That makes *me* older."

"I was born in the past," Lewis reminded him, "which makes *me* older!"

They struggled back and forth until the Time Machine spiraled out of control and plummeted to the ground.

Chapter 4

"**S**omebody's gonna have to fix this," stated Lewis. He and Wilbur were staring at the wrecked Time Machine lying on the ground.

"Good idea!" Wilbur replied as he pointed directly at Lewis.

"Are you crazy? I can't fix this thing!" blurted Lewis.

But Wilbur wouldn't take no for an answer. So Lewis offered him a deal: If Lewis fixed the Time

Machine, Wilbur would take Lewis to see his mom.

Wilbur had no choice. Reluctantly, he agreed.

Together they pushed the smoldering Time Machine into the Robinsons' garage. Carl, the Robinsons' faithful family robot, took one look at Lewis, shrieked, and ran away.

"That was unexpected," said Lewis.

Then Wilbur plopped a funny fruit hat onto Lewis's head.

". . . as was that," Lewis added.

"If my family finds out I brought you from the past,

they'll bury me alive and dance on my grave," he said. "I'm not exaggerating! Well, yes I am. But that's not the point. The point is, your hair's a dead give-away that you're from the past." And Carl had already seen Lewis. Not off to a good start.

"Why is my hair a dead giveaway?" asked Lewis.

"That is an excellent question." Wilbur darted to the far end of the garage and stood underneath a clear Travel Tube.

"Wait! Where are you going?" cried Lewis, seeing that Wilbur was headed in the same direction as Carl.

"Another excellent question!" Wilbur replied. And he wasn't going to answer it. He told Lewis to stay put, and he shot upward, zooming away to find Carl. The robot had the blueprints that would guide Lewis in fixing the Time Machine.

Wilbur tried to calm Carl—not an easy task when you're dealing with a hysterical robot.

"By leaving the garage door unlocked you let the Time Machine get stolen, and now the entire time stream could be altered!" exclaimed Carl. "There's a 99.999999 percent chance that you won't exist," Carl calculated.

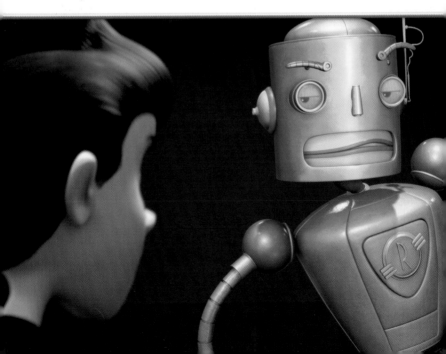

"I won't exist?" Wilbur was shocked. But he wasn't worried. After all, Wilbur Robinson never fails! At least that's what Wilbur liked to tell himself. He thanked Carl for the Time Machine blueprints and headed back to the garage.

But the garage was empty.

Lewis wasn't there. And that was bad. Extremely bad.

Wilbur had to find Lewis. Fast.

Chapter 5

Lewis's curiosity got the better of him. Standing near another Travel Tube in the garage, he had accidentally been sucked inside, and after a wild ride had landed on the Robinsons' front lawn. That's where he met Wilbur's eccentric Grandpa Bud. Grandpa liked to wear his clothes backwards and had spent all day looking for his false teeth. Lewis had agreed to help Grandpa Bud find his teeth

if Bud would help Lewis find his way back to the garage. But they were completely lost. They wandered into the train room and met Aunt Billie, who invented giant toy trains, and Uncle Gaston, who invented cannons—like the ones from which he launched himself when he raced against Billie's trains. Lewis met Uncle Joe, who "worked out" by watching exercise shows on TV, and Uncle Art, the intergalactic pizza delivery guy. Cousin Laszlo had been flying with his helicopter helmet to paint the top of his sister Tallulah's very fashionably tall hat when their dad, Uncle Fritz, appeared with

his puppet wife, Petunia. They'd seen Lefty, the octopuslike butler, and Grandma, Bud's beloved dancing wife.

Now Lewis and Grandpa were in the music room, where Wilbur's mother, Franny, conducted her frog orchestra. And the lead singer, Frankie the frog, had Grandpa's teeth!

As the whole family rushed in to celebrate the found teeth, Lewis sneaked away. He had to get back to the garage!

That's when he finally ran into Wilbur, who dragged him away from the others.

"Pop quiz. Who have you met and what have you learned?" Wilbur demanded.

Lewis explained how he had met the entire family.

"And nobody realized you were from the past?" Wilbur demanded.

"Nope," Lewis answered.

Wilbur sighed with relief. Now it was time to fix the broken Time Machine. While Lewis labored to repair it, Wilbur talked about his dad, Cornelius Robinson, Founder of the Future and president of his own invention company.

"Story time," Wilbur said as he started to pace. "Five years ago, Dad wakes up in the middle of the night in a cold sweat. He wants to build a Time Machine. So he starts working. We're talking plans. We're talking scale models. We're talking prototypes!" Wilbur emphasized how his dad had met failure after failure but didn't give up. In fact, his motto was "Keep moving forward."

Just a little more convincing, and Lewis would be in the palm of Wilbur's hand. Problem: Lewis looked ridiculous. "Dude, I can't take you seriously

in that hat." Wilbur took the fruit hat off Lewis's
head, replacing it with a baseball cap. There. He
could continue now. "He keeps working and working until finally . . . he gets it!"

Wilbur prepared for his grand finale, pointing
to the first working Time Machine and then to a
scale model of the second working Time Machine. It
looked no bigger than a toy.

"Kind of small," Lewis said.

Wilbur sighed. "I'm assuming that's a joke," he
said, disgruntled. "This, my friend, is merely a model
because, unfortunately, Time Machine number two is

in the hands of the Bowler Hat Guy!"

The story made an impact on Lewis. *Keep moving forward.* Sure enough, within a few hours he seemed to have succeeded in fixing the Time Machine. At least he *thought* he had fixed it.

Almost as quickly as it started up, the Time Machine smoked and sputtered and collapsed, worse than it was before. This time, however, Wilbur couldn't seem to help Lewis overcome his lack of confidence.

"It's over, okay? I can't do it!" Lewis said, walking away from his failed repair job.

Chapter 6

"**B**oys! Dinner time!" Franny called down to the garage.

At the dinner table, Lewis couldn't help feeling sad. He had failed again!

"Ladies and gentlemen, dinner is served!" Carl announced. Several mini Carls popped out of his chest delivering plates of meatballs. "Dinner is served! Dinner is served!" they said.

Wilbur couldn't help but notice Lewis

droop his head sadly.

Carl signaled to Wilbur. "Time to talk?"

Wilbur ducked down and quickly met with Carl under the table.

Carl began his irritating speech. "Why's the kid still here? Any of this ring a bell? Science fair. Memory Scanner. A time stream that needs fixing?!"

"Temporary setback," Wilbur mumbled. "He's just having a little confidence issue."

"Want me to talk to him?" Carl asked eagerly.

"No!" Wilbur knew he had to do this alone. "I've got it under control."

Wilbur returned to the table to find that the topic of conversation had turned to Lewis. Wilbur *had* to distract his family. They were paying way too much attention to Lewis. So he started a meatball fight. When it was all over, the entire Robinson clan was cheering and clapping . . . and still a bit hungry.

That's when Carl appeared wearing a strange contraption. Lewis gasped. It looked like one of Lewis's own inventions—the Peanut-Butter-and-Jelly Sandwich Maker!

"Okay, gang!" Carl said cheerily. "Time for

the second course. What goes better with meatballs than PB&J?"

Carl quickly began making sandwiches, but then the machine jammed.

"Carl, is everything all right?"

"We're just experiencing a few clogs here," Carl answered as he shook the peanut-butter-and-jelly squirters.

Wilbur's eyes lit up. "Just what the doctor ordered," he muttered to himself. Then he announced to the family, "My friend Lewis is an inventor! He can fix it!"

"Wilbur!" Lewis looked at his new so-called friend in disbelief. After all Lewis's failures, how could Wilbur set him up like this? "How am I—? *I can't!*"

But the family insisted he give it a try.

"You'd really be helping us out, Lewis," Franny pleaded. So Lewis tried to fix it—which he did. Too well. Peanut butter and jelly didn't just start oozing from the machine. It exploded from the machine. The whole room—the whole family—was covered in peanut butter and jelly.

"Oh, no! I'm sorry! I'm so sorry!" Lewis was devastated—until the family began congratulating him.

"From failing, you learn!" cried Aunt Billie. "From success? Mmm—not so much."

"If I gave up every time I failed, I never would've made the meatball cannon!" Uncle Gaston said proudly.

To the Robinsons, failure was good as long as you tried again. It meant that the next attempt on the next prototype would be even better! Lewis couldn't help smiling as the family toasted his failure by dumping their drinks on their heads.

"Gosh, you're all so nice," Lewis said. "If I

had a family, I—I'd want them to be just like you."

As the family celebrated, Franny caught up with Wilbur and asked him about Lewis. "What did he mean—*if* he had a family?"

"Um, Lewis is an orphan," Wilbur replied. But there was no time for explanations because just then the room began to shake. Wilbur stared out the window. For a moment, he couldn't believe his eyes—a Tyrannosaurus rex was crashing through it!

Chapter 7

Lurking outside, Bowler Hat Guy was controlling the dinosaur's mind with Little Doris, a mini version of his bowler hat. Doris had given the mini version of herself to Bowler Hat Guy to keep him occupied while she flew around looking for Lewis.

But Little Doris did more than keep Bowler Hat Guy entertained. Her tiny camera conveyed everything that she saw and heard to Bowler Hat Guy!

She could also control the mind of any living being upon whose head she perched. And now the dinosaur (with Little Doris on its head) sucked Lewis into its mouth.

The Robinson family really kicked into gear. Aunt Billie charged her giant toy train into the dinosaur's stomach.

"Choo-choo on this!" she shouted.

"Lewis!" shouted Wilbur as the dino spat the boy out of his mouth.

"Ready, aim, fire!" Uncle Gaston shot Lefty the butler out of his cannon toward the dinosaur. Lefty cleverly wrapped his octopus tentacles around the dino's head, freeing Lewis.

"Gotcha!" Uncle Art flashed a grin as he flew over to catch Lewis in his spaceship.

But despite the family's best efforts, soon Lewis was cornered. That's when the dinosaur ducked . . . and then Wilbur saw it: the tiny bowler hat on the creature's head.

"Bowler Hat Guy!" Wilbur gasped. He

quickly deduced that the villain was behind the dinosaur attack. Wilbur knew he needed to knock Little Doris off the dinosaur's head. The dinosaur tried to get Lewis but started to gobble up Wilbur instead!

Then Wilbur got the shock of his life. Lewis grabbed a shovel, catapulted himself into the dinosaur's mouth and wedged it between the dinosaur's menacing jaws. Awesome! The T. rex couldn't close its mouth! Wilbur grabbed Uncle Gaston's meatball shooter, which had been wedged between the dinosaur's teeth, and aimed carefully. A meatball ricocheted off the house and knocked Little Doris off the dinosaur's head.

No longer under the mind control of Bowler Hat Guy, the dinosaur toppled.

"Are you boys all right?" Franny cried. She wasn't quite sure what had happened.

"Did you see us take out that dinosaur?" Lewis said. "It was so cool!"

Franny smiled at Lewis. "I'm really happy you're safe." She pulled Lewis into a hug.

Wilbur snapped into action. "We really have to go."

"Lewis?" said Franny. "Do you want to be . . . a Robinson?"

"Y-you want to adopt me?" Lewis couldn't believe his ears. He was overjoyed.

Wilbur gulped. He didn't have a choice. He reached over and knocked the baseball cap off Lewis's head, exposing his hair. The Robinsons gasped.

"Okay," Lewis said. "It's true. I'm from the past. Now you know the big secret."

"Lewis, I am so sorry," Franny said quickly. "But you have to go."

Lewis was heartbroken. Then he remembered something.

"Wait!" he said. "If I have to leave, can I at least go back and find my mom? Wilbur promised."

Franny looked at Wilbur angrily. "You promised *what*?!" she asked.

"I was never going to do it!" Wilbur cried without thinking. "I swear!" Realizing what he had said, he clamped his hand over his mouth.

"You lied to me?!" Lewis demanded. "I can't believe I was dumb enough to actually believe you were my friend." He turned and ran.

Sitting in the Robinsons' garden sobbing, Lewis heard an odd voice.

"Oh, yes, Doris, it is a shame. All he wants to do is go back in time and meet the mother he never knew."

A Time Machine appeared before Lewis, and inside was . . .

"Bowler Hat Guy?" Lewis gasped.

"Hello, Lewis," Bowler Hat Guy said. Then he made an offer: Lewis would fix the broken Memory Scanner, and Bowler Hat Guy and Doris would take

Lewis back to find his birth mother in the Time Machine.

Wilbur, meanwhile, was racing to find Lewis. The kid was in serious danger and didn't even know it! "Lewis!" Wilbur shouted. "Lewis! Let's just talk about this, Lewis. I know you're around here somewhere."

But by the time Wilbur found Lewis, he was flying away in the Time Machine with Bowler Hat Guy.

Chapter 8

"**I** can't imagine why you're so interested in this piece of junk," Lewis said as he worked on the Memory Scanner. Bowler Hat Guy had taken him across town to a deserted building.

Lewis held up his end up the deal. He fixed it. But then the villain revealed he had been hiding one hand behind his back—with crossed fingers. "Crossies! Doesn't count!" Bowler Hat Guy cried

out, delighted that he had gotten away with it. He wasn't going to take Lewis to meet his mom!

"Why are you doing this to me?" Lewis asked.

The not-so-bright Bowler Hat Guy was feeling very clever. "You still haven't figured it out?"

"Figured what out?" Lewis said, frowning in confusion.

"Well, let's see if this rings a bell," Bowler Hat Guy said. "Founder of the Future, inventor extraordinaire, keep moving forward . . ."

"That's not me. That's Wilbur's dad," Lewis said.

Bowler Hat Guy flashed his best villain glare.

Lewis's eyes went round. "Are you saying that *I'm* Wilbur's dad?" he cried.

"You grow up to be the founder of this wretched time," Bowler Hat Guy explained. "So I plan to destroy your destiny. Easy peasy, rice and cheesy."

"So, if I'm Wilbur's dad," Lewis thought aloud, "what does that have to do with you?"

"Allow me to shed some light on the subject," Bowler Hat Guy said, switching on an overhead light bulb.

Lewis looked around. "My old room?"

"I think you mean *our* old room!" Bowler Hat Guy cried.

Lewis finally realized that the bitter man standing before him was his old roommate, Goob, from the orphanage. "How'd you end up like this?" Lewis asked.

"Well," Bowler Hat Guy began, "it's a long and pitiful story of a young boy with a dream—a dream of winning a championship baseball game— a dream that was ruined in the last inning. We lost by one run because of me."

Bowler Hat Guy sorrowfully remembered his

childhood and missing the winning catch because he fell asleep. While Lewis had been adopted, become famous, and gone on to lead a happy, successful life, the embittered boy in the scrawny baseball uniform had grown into adulthood alone in the orphanage, long after it had closed down.

"It was then that I finally realized it wasn't my fault!" Bowler Hat Guy shouted at Lewis. "It was yours! If you hadn't kept me up all night working on your stupid science fair project, then I wouldn't have fallen asleep and missed the catch. So I devised a brilliant plan to get my revenge." Bowler Hat Guy sneered.

His revenge? He had thrown eggs at the Robinson Industries building. And there he had met Doris—one of Robinson Industries' rejected inventions—and the two of them formed the perfect evil duo. Together they plotted to steal the Time Machine, go back to the science fair, take Lewis's science project—the Memory Scanner that had made him famous—and pass it off as his own!

"Look, I'm sorry your life turned out so bad,"

Lewis said, "but don't blame me! You messed it up yourself. You just focused on the bad stuff when all you had to do was let go of the past . . ." Lewis realized, remembering the Robinsons' motto. "And keep moving forward!"

But Bowler Hat Guy preferred to blame Lewis for everything. He took Lewis and the Memory Scanner to the roof of the abandoned orphanage, laughing villainously.

"This is going to be the best day of my life!" he shouted. He would pass off the Memory Scanner invention as his own and ruin Lewis's future!

Little did he know that Wilbur had figured out where Lewis was! And at that very moment, Wilbur and Carl were at the edge of the rooftop waiting to save Lewis. Carl had extended his robotic legs so that he was as tall as the roof!

"Coo! Coo!" Wilbur signaled to Lewis.

Lewis instinctively knew just what to do. He pushed the wagon carrying the Memory Scanner over the edge of the roof and leaped into Carl's arms, joining Wilbur.

"Well, I hate to foil your evil plan and run," Carl said as Bowler Hat Guy and Doris were just climbing into their Time Machine, "but . . . ta-ta!" And, boy, could Carl run on his hyper-extended robot legs.

"I bet you're glad to see me!" Wilbur said to Lewis, but Lewis punched him in the arm. "Ow!"

"That's for not locking the garage door!" Lewis said.

"You know about that?" Wilbur asked, shocked.

"I know everything," Lewis replied. He had learned an awful lot from Bowler Hat Guy.

Just then the Robinsons' home came into view. "Ha-ha!" cried Carl. "Look at that, boys! We're almost home free!" *Ka-thunk*. Carl collapsed. Doris had shot a grappling hook through his chest. She and Bowler Hat Guy had caught up with them in the Time Machine. Then Doris grabbed the Memory Scanner and flew back to Bowler Hat Guy.

"Take a good look around, boys, because your future is about to change!" Bowler Hat Guy shouted as he flew away. Now, at last, he could go back to Lewis's time, pass off the Memory Scanner as his own invention, and take over Lewis's destiny to become Founder of the Future and

the most famous inventor.

"Lewis, you have to fix the Time Machine!" Wilbur shouted. He was getting desperate. They were running out of time. The entire future—even Wilbur's existence—was at stake.

"No, no! I—I can't!" Lewis looked terrified. "What about your dad? You could call him!"

"You *are* my dad!" Wilbur pushed forward. He needed Lewis—his dad—to understand. Lewis had to fix the Time Machine, follow Doris and Bowler Hat Guy back in time, and foil their plans

to change the future.

"There won't be a future unless you fix this Time Machine," Wilbur pleaded. "Look, I messed up. I left the garage unlocked, and I've tried like crazy to fix things. But now it's up to you. You can do it, Dad!" The world around them started spinning and turning gray. "Lewis?" Wilbur was scared. A huge swirling vortex appeared in the sky. "Lewwwisss!" Wilbur shouted as he was swept up into the sky.

Wilbur heard Lewis yelling, "Wilburrrr!" just before all went black.

Chapter 9

Wilbur had to give the kid credit. Somehow Lewis—er, his dad—managed to pull it off. Wilbur was lost in oblivion because the future was changing, thanks to Bowler Hat Guy and Doris. Meanwhile, Lewis saw the alternate, evil future and learned that it was all Doris's vision—not Bowler Hat Guy's! It had been her plan all along.

Lewis had fixed the broken Time Machine,

gone back in time, and stopped Bowler Hat Guy from changing the future forever. He told Bowler Hat Guy that Doris was just using him and would dump him after she created her horrible vision of a future. Although evil, Bowler Hat Guy only wanted to destroy Lewis's destiny, not the future itself.

And when Doris attacked Lewis, he yelled, "I am *never* going to invent you," and Doris was gone. Forever.

"Hey, you did it, Lewis!" Wilbur shouted, now happily back in the future at the Robinsons' house.

Then Wilbur saw Bowler Hat Guy in the Time Machine with Lewis.

"He's my roommate," Lewis said, but as he took Wilbur aside to explain, Bowler Hat Guy sneaked away. It was time for Goob to find his own destiny.

Soon all the Robinsons gathered around the boys, happy to see them safe and sound. Franny was the first to hug Lewis. "Are you hurt? Any broken bones?"

The other family members seemed just as concerned.

Wilbur smiled. It had all worked out perfectly. Almost.

"Franny?" came a voice from the garage. "They're gone!"

Uh-oh. Wilbur's dad, Cornelius, had finally come home. Wilbur knew he would be grounded now for the rest of his life. Instead, Cornelius surprised everyone. He didn't seem to mind meeting his past self. In fact, he took Lewis on a tour of his invention lab.

"Hey, want to see the one I'm the most

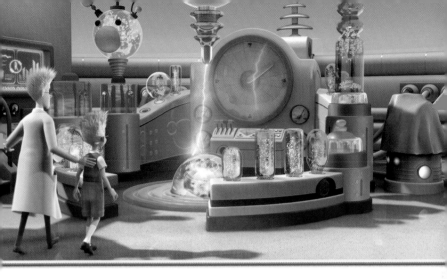

proud of?" asked Cornelius. He pulled a cover off an old invention. It was the Memory Scanner.

"It was our first real invention," Cornelius told Lewis. "It's the one that started it all."

"Wowee!" Lewis cried. "So if I go back now, then this'll be my future!"

"Well," said Cornelius thoughtfully, "that depends on you. Nothing is set in stone. You gotta make the right choices and keep moving forward."

The Robinsons shouted good-bye as Lewis, with Wilbur at the controls, flew away in the Time Machine. Lewis had to smile, knowing that Grandma Lucille and Grandpa Bud would soon become his parents . . . in the past!

Chapter 10

"**W**ait a minute. You're supposed to take me back to the science fair," said Lewis as they landed in front of the orphanage. "I think you punched in the wrong numbers."

"We agreed that I'd take you back to see your mom," Wilbur said, keeping his promise. But when Lewis saw the woman leaving the baby at the orphanage steps, he decided not to meet her.

"I don't get it," Wilbur said as he dropped Lewis back off at the orphanage rooftop. "You wanted to meet her so bad. Why did you just let her go?"

Lewis smiled. "Because," he said, "I'm your

dad." And Lewis wanted to make sure that the future stayed just the way it was, and that he would one day become a part of the Robinson family. He had seen his future family. And he had liked them. A lot.

"I never thought my dad would be my best friend," Wilbur sighed. The boy from the future hesitated and then climbed into the Time Machine. "You got that motto?" he asked. He meant "Keep moving forward."

Lewis nodded. "I got it."

"Don't forget it," Wilbur said.

"I don't think that's possible," Lewis told him.

He turned away with the Memory Scanner. "See ya later, Wilbur!"

Then Lewis returned to the science fair, but not before waking Goob in time to make the winning catch. This time, the Memory Scanner worked, and Dr. Krunklehorn remembered her marriage to . . . Bud Robinson. Grandpa Bud?! Sure enough, the couple soon fell in love with Lewis and adopted him.

Lewis changed his name to Cornelius Robinson, knowing one day he would become a famous inventor and the Founder of the Future. But most importantly, he became part of a family. The coolest family in the whole world.